The Hunting of the Snark

The Hunting of the Snark

AN AGONY IN EIGHT FITS
by LEWIS CARROLL

Illustrated by Mahendra Singh

MELVILLEHOUSE
BROOKLYN, NEW YORK

THE HUNTING OF THE SNARK
© 2010 Melville House Publishing

Illustrations © 2010 Mahendra Singh

First Melville House printing: September 2010

Melville House Publishing
145 Plymouth Street
Brooklyn, NY 11201

www.mhpbooks.com

ISBN: 978-1-935554-24-0

Printed in the United States of America

1 2 3 4 5 6 7 8 9 10

Library of Congress Control Number: 2010936527

AUTHOR'S DEDICATION & POEM

*Inscribed to a dear Child: in memory of golden
summer hours and whispers of a summer sea.*

Girt with a boyish garb for boyish task,
Eager she wields her spade: yet loves as well
Rest on a friendly knee, intent to ask
The tale he loves to tell.

Rude spirits of the seething outer strife,
Unmeet to read her pure and simple spright,
Deem, if you list, such hours a waste of life,
Empty of all delight!

Chat on, sweet Maid, and rescue from annoy
Hearts that by wiser talk are unbeguiled.
Ah, happy he who owns that tenderest joy,
The heart-love of a child!

Away, fond thoughts, and vex my soul no more!
Work claims my wakeful nights, my busy days—
Albeit bright memories of that sunlit shore
Yet haunt my dreaming gaze!

ARTIST'S DEDICATION

—◆•◆—

With forks and hope and love for Yamini

FIG. I — A visual explication of the portmanteau concept. Shown here is the celebrated poet and author of this preface, Lewis Carroll, with a portmanteau of the Rev. Charles Lutwidge Dodgson, mathematics don at Christ Church College.

Preface

BY LEWIS CARROLL

If—and the thing is wildly possible—the charge of writing nonsense were ever brought against the author of this brief but instructive poem, it would be based, I feel convinced, on the line (in Fit the Second)

"Then the bowsprit got mixed with the rudder sometimes."

In view of this painful possibility, I will not (as I might) appeal indignantly to my other writings as a proof that I am incapable of such a deed: I will not (as I might) point to the strong moral purpose of this poem itself, to the arithmetical principles so cautiously inculcated in it, or to its noble teachings in Natural History—I will take the more prosaic course of simply explaining how it happened.

The Bellman, who was almost morbidly sensitive about appearances, used to have the bowsprit unshipped once or twice a week to be revarnished, and it more than once happened, when the time came for replacing it, that no one on board could remember which end of the ship it belonged to. They knew it was not of the slightest use to appeal to the Bellman about it—he would only refer to his Naval Code, and read out in pathetic tones Admiralty Instructions which none of them had ever been able to understand—so it generally ended in its being fastened on, anyhow, across the rudder. The helmsman* used to stand by with tears in his eyes; *he* knew it was all wrong, but alas! Rule 42 of the Code, *"No one shall speak to the*

---

*This office was usually undertaken by the Boots, who found in it a refuge from the Baker's constant complaints about the insufficient blacking of his three pairs of boots.

Man at the Helm," had been completed by the Bellman himself with the words *"and the Man at the Helm shall speak to no one."* So remonstrance was impossible, and no steering could be done till the next varnishing day. During these bewildering intervals the ship usually sailed backwards.

As this poem is to some extent connected with the lay of the Jabberwock, let me take this opportunity of answering a question that has often been asked me, how to pronounce "slithy toves." The "i" in "slithy" is long, as in "writhe"; and "toves" is pronounced so as to rhyme with "groves." Again, the first "o" in "borogoves" is pronounced like the "o" in "borrow." I have heard people try to give it the sound of the "o" in "worry." Such is Human Perversity.

This also seems a fitting occasion to notice the other hard words in that poem. Humpty-Dumpty's theory, of two meanings packed into one word like a portmanteau, seems to me the right explanation for all.

For instance, take the two words "fuming" and "furious." Make up your mind that you will say both words, but leave it unsettled which you will say first. Now open your mouth and speak. If your thoughts incline ever so little towards "fuming," you will say "fuming-furious"; if they turn, by even a hair's breadth, towards "furious," you will say "furious-fuming"; but if you have that rarest of gifts, a perfectly balanced mind, you will say "frumious."

Supposing that, when Pistol uttered the well-known words —
"Under which king, Bezonian? Speak or die!"
Justice Shallow had felt certain that it was either William or Richard, but had not been able to settle which, so that he could not possibly say either name before the other, can it be doubted that, rather than die, he would have gasped out "Rilchiam!"

FIG. 2 — A visual explication of the portmanteau concept. Shown here is the Christ Church mathematics don, the Rev. Charles Lutwidge Dodgson, with a portmanteau of Lewis Carroll, the celebrated poet and the author of this preface.

Fit the First
THE LANDING

"Just the place for a Snark!" the Bellman cried,
As he landed his crew with care;
Supporting each man on the top of the tide
By a finger entwined in his hair.

"Just the place for a Snark! I have said it twice:
That alone should encourage the crew.
Just the place for a Snark! I have said it thrice:
What I tell you three times is true."

The crew was complete: it included a Boots—
A maker of Bonnets and Hoods—
A Barrister, brought to arrange their disputes—
And a Broker, to value their goods.

A Billiard-marker, whose skill was immense,
Might perhaps have won more than his share—
But a Banker, engaged at enormous expense,
Had the whole of their cash in his care.
There was also a Beaver, that paced on the deck,
Or would sit making lace in the bow:
And had often (the Bellman said) saved them from wreck,
Though none of the sailors knew how.

There was one who was famed for the number of things
He forgot when he entered the ship:
His umbrella, his watch, all his jewels and rings,
And the clothes he had bought for the trip.

He had forty-two boxes, all carefully packed,
With his name painted clearly on each:
But, since he omitted to mention the fact,
They were all left behind on the beach.
The loss of his clothes hardly mattered, because
He had seven coats on when he came,
With three pairs of boots—but the worst of it was,
He had wholly forgotten his name.

He would answer to "Hi!" or to any loud cry,
Such as "Fry me!" or "Fritter my wig!"
To "What-you-may-call-um!" or "What-was-his-name!"
But especially "Thing-um-a-jig!"
While, for those who preferred a more forcible word,
He had different names from these:
His intimate friends called him "Candle-ends,"
And his enemies "Toasted-cheese."

"His form is ungainly—his intellect small—"
(So the Bellman would often remark)
"But his courage is perfect! And that, after all,
Is the thing that one needs with a Snark."
He would joke with hyænas, returning their stare
With an impudent wag of the head:
And he once went a walk, paw-in-paw, with a bear,
"Just to keep up its spirits," he said.

He came as a Baker: but owned, when too late—
And it drove the poor Bellman half-mad—
He could only bake Bridecake—for which, I may state,
No materials were to be had.

The last of the crew needs especial remark,
Though he looked an incredible dunce:
He had just one idea—but, that one being "Snark,"
The good Bellman engaged him at once.

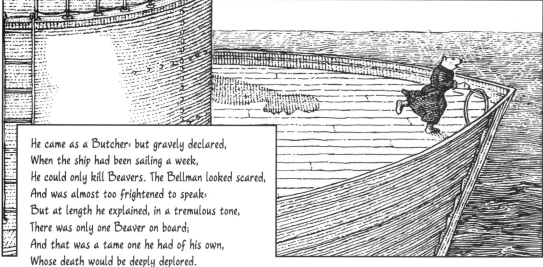

He came as a Butcher: but gravely declared,
When the ship had been sailing a week,
He could only kill Beavers. The Bellman looked scared,
And was almost too frightened to speak:
But at length he explained, in a tremulous tone,
There was only one Beaver on board;
And that was a tame one he had of his own,
Whose death would be deeply deplored.

The Beaver, who happened to hear the remark,
Protested, with tears in its eyes,
That not even the rapture of hunting the Snark
Could atone for that dismal surprise!
It strongly advised that the Butcher should be
Conveyed in a separate ship:
But the Bellman declared that would never agree
With the plans he had made for the trip:
Navigation was always a difficult art,
Though with only one ship and one bell:
And he feared he must really decline, for his part,
Undertaking another as well.

The Beaver's best course was, no doubt, to procure
A second-hand dagger-proof coat—
So the Baker advised it—and next, to insure
Its life in some Office of note:
This the Banker suggested, and offered for hire
(On moderate terms), or for sale,
Two excellent Policies, one Against Fire,
And one Against Damage From Hail.

Yet still, ever after that sorrowful day,
Whenever the Butcher was by,
The Beaver kept looking the opposite way,
And appeared unaccountably shy.

Fit the Second

THE BELLMAN'S SPEECH

The Bellman himself they all
praised to the skies—
Such a carriage, such ease
and such grace!
Such solemnity, too!
One could see he was wise,
The moment one looked
in his face!

He had bought a large map representing the sea,
Without the least vestige of land:
And the crew were much pleased when they found it to be
A map they could all understand.

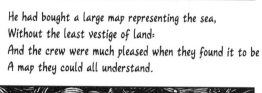

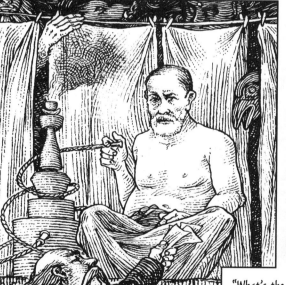

vous êtes
ici toujours

"What's the good of Mercator's North Poles and Equators,
Tropics, Zones, and Meridian Lines?"
So the Bellman would cry: and the crew would reply
"They are merely conventional signs!

"Other maps are such shapes, with their islands and capes!
But we've got our brave Captain to thank"
(So the crew would protest) "that he's bought us the best—
A perfect and absolute blank!"

This was charming, no doubt:
  but they shortly found out
That the Captain they trusted so well
Had only one notion for
  crossing the ocean,
And that was to tingle his bell.

He was thoughtful and grave—
  but the orders he gave
Were enough to bewilder a crew.
When he cried "Steer to starboard,
  but keep her head larboard!"
What on earth was the
  helmsman to do?
Then the bowsprit got mixed
  with the rudder sometimes:
A thing, as the Bellman remarked,
That frequently happens
  in tropical climes,
When a vessel is, so to speak, "snarked."

But the principal failing
  occurred in the sailing,
And the Bellman,
  perplexed and distressed,
Said he *had* hoped, at least,
  when the wind blew due East,
That the ship would *not*
  travel due West!

But the danger was past—they had landed at last,
With their boxes, portmanteaus, and bags:
Yet at first sight the crew were not pleased with the view,
Which consisted of chasms and crags.

The Bellman perceived that their spirits were low,
And repeated in musical tone
Some jokes he had kept for a season of woe—
But the crew would do nothing but groan.

He served out some grog
    with a liberal hand,
And bade them sit down on the beach:
And they could not but own that their
    Captain looked grand,
As he stood and delivered his speech.
"Friends, Romans, and countrymen,
    lend me your ears!"
(They were all of them fond of quotations:
So they drank to his health, and
    they gave him three cheers,
While he served out additional rations).

"We have sailed many months, we have sailed many weeks,
    (Four weeks to the month you may mark),
    But never as yet ('tis your Captain who speaks)
    Have we caught the least glimpse of a Snark!

"We have sailed many weeks,
  we have sailed many days,
(Seven days to the week I allow),
But a Snark, on the which we
  might lovingly gaze,
We have never beheld till now!
"Come, listen, my men,
  while I tell you again
The five unmistakable marks
By which you may know,
  wheresoever you go,
The warranted genuine Snarks.

fig. 1

"Let us take them in order.
  The first is the taste,
Which is meager and hollow, but crisp:
Like a coat that is rather too
  tight in the waist,
With a flavour of Will-o-the-wisp.

"Its habit of getting up late you'll agree
That it carries too far, when I say
That it frequently breakfasts at five-o'clock tea,
And dines on the following day.

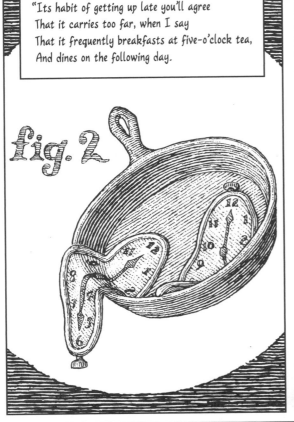

fig. 2

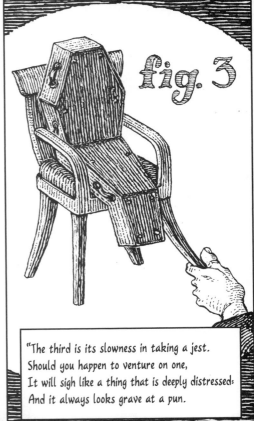

fig. 3

"The third is its slowness in taking a jest.
Should you happen to venture on one,
It will sigh like a thing that is deeply distressed:
And it always looks grave at a pun.

"The fourth is its fondness for bathing-machines,
Which it constantly carries about,
And believes that they add to the beauty of scenes—
A sentiment open to doubt.

fig. 4

fig. 5

"The fifth is ambition. It next will be right
To describe each particular batch:
Distinguishing those that have feathers, and bite,
From those that have whiskers, and scratch.

"For, although common Snarks do no manner of harm,
Yet, I feel it my duty to say,
Some are Boojums—" The Bellman broke off in alarm,
For the Baker had fainted away.

Fit the Third

THE BAKER'S TALE

They roused him with muffins—
  they roused him with ice—
They roused him with mustard and cress—
They roused him with jam and
  judicious advice—
They set him conundrums to guess.

When at length he sat up and was able to speak,
His sad story he offered to tell;
And the Bellman cried "Silence! Not even a shriek!"
And excitedly tingled his bell.
There was silence supreme! Not a shriek, not a scream,
Scarcely even a howl or a groan,
As the man they called "Ho!" told his story of woe
In an antediluvian tone.

"My father and mother were honest, though poor—"
"Skip all that!" cried the Bellman in haste.
"If it once becomes dark, there's no chance of a Snark—
   We have hardly a minute to waste!"

"I skip forty years," said the Baker, in tears,
"And proceed without further remark
 To the day when you took me aboard of your ship
 To help you in hunting the Snark.

"A dear uncle of mine (after whom I was named)
   Remarked, when I bade him farewell—"
"Oh, skip your dear uncle!" the Bellman exclaimed,
   As he angrily tingled his bell.

"He remarked to me then," said that mildest of men,
" 'If your Snark be a Snark, that is right:
Fetch it home by all means—you may serve it with greens,
And it's handy for striking a light.

" 'You may seek it with thimbles—and seek it with care;
You may hunt it with forks and hope;
You may threaten its life with a railway-share;
You may charm it with smiles and soap—' "

("That's exactly the method," the Bellman bold
In a hasty parenthesis cried,
"That's exactly the way I have always been told
That the capture of Snarks should be tried!")

" 'But oh, beamish nephew, beware of the day,
If your Snark be a Boojum! For then
You will softly and suddenly vanish away,
And never be met with again!'
"It is this, it is this that oppresses my soul,
When I think of my uncle's last words:
And my heart is like nothing so much as a bowl
Brimming over with quivering curds!

"It is this, it is this—" "We have had that before!"
The Bellman indignantly said.
And the Baker replied "Let me say it once more.
It is this, it is this that I dread!

"I engage with the Snark—every night after dark—
In a dreamy delirious fight:
I serve it with greens in those shadowy scenes,
And I use it for striking a light:

"But if ever I meet with a Boojum, that day,
In a moment (of this I am sure),
I shall softly and suddenly vanish away—
And the notion I cannot endure!"

Fit the Fourth

THE HUNTING

The Bellman looked uffish, and wrinkled his brow.
"If only you'd spoken before!
It's excessively awkward to mention it now,
With the Snark, so to speak, at the door!
"We should all of us grieve, as you well may believe,
If you never were met with again—
But surely, my man, when the voyage began,
You might have suggested it then?

"It's excessively awkward to mention it now—
As I think I've already remarked."
And the man they called "Hi!" replied, with a sigh,
"I informed you the day we embarked.

"The rest of my speech" (he explained to his men)
"You shall hear when I've leisure to speak it.
But the Snark is at hand, let me tell you again!
'Tis your glorious duty to seek it!

"To seek it with thimbles, to seek it with care;
To pursue it with forks and hope;
To threaten its life with a railway-share;
To charm it with smiles and soap!

"For the Snark's a peculiar creature, that won't
Be caught in a commonplace way.
Do all that you know, and try all that you don't:
Not a chance must be wasted to-day!

"For England expects—I forbear to proceed:
'Tis a maxim tremendous, but trite:
And you'd best be unpacking the things that you need
To rig yourselves out for the fight."

Then the Banker endorsed a blank cheque (which he crossed),
And changed his loose silver for notes.
The Baker with care combed his whiskers and hair,
And shook the dust out of his coats.

The Boots and the Broker were sharpening a spade—
Each working the grindstone in turn:
But the Beaver went on making lace, and displayed
No interest in the concern:

Though the Barrister tried to appeal to its pride,
And vainly proceeded to cite
A number of cases, in which making laces
Had been proved an infringement of right.

The maker of Bonnets ferociously planned
A novel arrangement of bows:
While the Billiard-marker with quivering hand
Was chalking the tip of his nose.

"Introduce me, now there's a good fellow," he said,
"If we happen to meet it together!"
And the Bellman, sagaciously nodding his head,
Said "That must depend on the weather."

But the Butcher turned nervous, and dressed himself fine,
With yellow kid gloves and a ruff—
Said he felt it exactly like going to dine,
Which the Bellman declared was all "stuff."

The Beaver went simply galumphing about,
At seeing the Butcher so shy:
And even the Baker, though stupid and stout,
Made an effort to wink with one eye.

"Be a man!" said the Bellman in wrath, as he heard
The Butcher beginning to sob.
"Should we meet with a Jubjub, that desperate bird,
We shall need all our strength for the job!"

Fit the Fifth
THE BEAVER'S LESSON

They sought it with thimbles, they sought it with care;
They pursued it with forks and hope,
They threatened its life with a railway-share;
They charmed it with smiles and soap.

Then the Butcher contrived an ingenious plan
For making a separate sally;
And had fixed on a spot unfrequented by man,
A dismal and desolate valley.

But the very same plan to the Beaver occurred:
It had chosen the very same place:
Yet neither betrayed, by a sign or a word,
The disgust that appeared in his face.

Each thought he was thinking of nothing but "Snark"
And the glorious work of the day;
And each tried to pretend that he did not remark
That the other was going that way.

But the valley grew narrow and narrower still,
And the evening got darker and colder,
Till (merely from nervousness, not from goodwill)
They marched along shoulder to shoulder.

Then a scream, shrill and high, rent the shuddering sky,
And they knew that some danger was near:
The Beaver turned pale to the tip of its tail,
And even the Butcher felt queer.

He thought of his childhood, left far far behind—
That blissful and innocent state—
The sound so exactly recalled to his mind
A pencil that squeaks on a slate!

"'Tis the voice of the Jubjub!" he suddenly cried.
(This man, that they used to call "Dunce.")
"As the Bellman would tell you," he added with pride,
"I have uttered that sentiment once.

"'Tis the note of the Jubjub! Keep count, I entreat;
You will find I have told it you twice.
'Tis the song of the Jubjub! The proof is complete,
If only I've stated it thrice."

The Beaver had counted with scrupulous care,
Attending to every word:
But it fairly lost heart, and
    outgrabe in despair,
When the third repetition occurred.

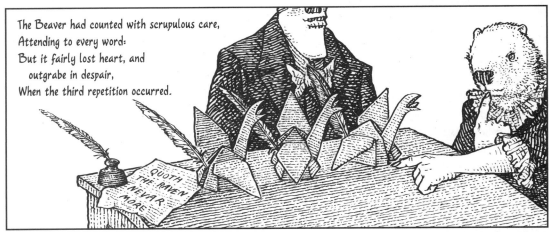

It felt that, in spite of all
        possible pains,
It had somehow contrived
        to lose count,
And the only thing now was to
        rack its poor brains
By reckoning up the amount.

"Two added to one—if that could but be done,"
It said, "with one's fingers and thumbs!"
Recollecting with tears how, in earlier years,
It had taken no pains with its sums.
"The thing can be done," said the Butcher, "I think.
The thing must be done, I am sure.
The thing shall be done! Bring me paper and ink,
The best there is time to procure."

The Beaver brought paper, portfolio, pens,
And ink in unfailing supplies:
While strange creepy creatures came out of their dens,
And watched them with wondering eyes.

So engrossed was the Butcher, he heeded them not,
As he wrote with a pen in each hand,
And explained all the while in a popular style
Which the Beaver could well understand.

"Taking Three as the subject to reason about—
A convenient number to state—
We add Seven, and Ten, and then multiply out
By One Thousand diminished by Eight.

"The result we proceed to divide, as you see,
By Nine Hundred and Ninety and Two:
Then subtract Seventeen, and the answer must be
Exactly and perfectly true.

"The method employed I would gladly explain,
While I have it so clear in my head,
If I had but the time and you had but the brain—
But much yet remains to be said.
"In one moment I've seen what has hitherto been
Enveloped in absolute mystery,
And without extra charge I will give you at large
A Lesson in Natural History."

In his genial way he proceeded to say
(Forgetting all laws of propriety,
And that giving instruction, without introduction,
Would have caused quite a thrill in Society),
"As to temper the Jubjub's a desperate bird,
Since it lives in perpetual passion:
Its taste in costume is entirely absurd —
It is ages ahead of the fashion:

"But it knows any friend it has met once before:
It never will look at a bribe:
And in charity-meetings it stands at the door,
And collects—though it does not subscribe.

"Its flavour when cooked is more exquisite far
Than mutton, or oysters, or eggs:
(Some think it keeps best in an ivory jar,
And some, in mahogany kegs:)

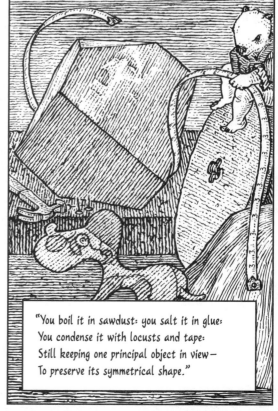

"You boil it in sawdust: you salt it in glue:
You condense it with locusts and tape:
Still keeping one principal object in view—
To preserve its symmetrical shape."

The Butcher would gladly have talked till next day,
But he felt that the Lesson must end,
And he wept with delight in attempting to say
He considered the Beaver his friend.

While the Beaver confessed, with affectionate looks
More eloquent even than tears,
It had learned in ten minutes far more than all books
Would have taught it in seventy years.
They returned hand-in-hand, and the Bellman, unmanned
(For a moment) with noble emotion,
Said "This amply repays all the wearisome days
We have spent on the billowy ocean!"

Such friends, as the Beaver and Butcher became,
Have seldom if ever been known;
In winter or summer, 'twas always the same—
You could never meet either alone.

And when quarrels arose—as one frequently finds
Quarrels will, spite of every endeavour—
The song of the Jubjub recurred to their minds,
And cemented their friendship for ever!

THE BARRISTER'S DREAM

They sought it with thimbles, they sought it with care;
They pursued it with forks and hope;
They threatened its life with a railway-share;
They charmed it with smiles and soap.

But the Barrister, weary of proving in vain
That the Beaver's lace-making was wrong,
Fell asleep, and in dreams saw the creature quite plain
That his fancy had dwelt on so long.

He dreamed that he stood in a shadowy Court,
Where the Snark, with a glass in its eye,
Dressed in gown, bands, and wig, was defending a pig
On the charge of deserting its sty.

The Witnesses proved, without error or flaw,
That the sty was deserted when found:
And the Judge kept explaining the state of the law
In a soft under-current of sound.

The indictment had never been clearly expressed,
And it seemed that the Snark had begun,
And had spoken three hours, before any one guessed
What the pig was supposed to have done.
The Jury had each formed a different view
(Long before the indictment was read),
And they all spoke at once, so that none of them knew
One word that the others had said.

"You must know—" said the Judge: but the Snark exclaimed "Fudge!
That statute is obsolete quite!
Let me tell you, my friends, the whole question depends
On an ancient manorial right.
"In the matter of Treason the pig would appear
To have aided, but scarcely abetted:
While the charge of Insolvency fails, it is clear,
If you grant the plea 'never indebted.'

"My poor client's fate now depends on your votes."
Here the speaker sat down in his place,
And directed the Judge to refer to his notes
And briefly to sum up the case.
But the Judge said he never had summed up before;
So the Snark undertook it instead,
And summed it so well that it came to far more
Than the Witnesses ever had said!

"The fact of Desertion I will not dispute:
But its guilt, as I trust, is removed
(So far as related to the costs of this suit)
By the Alibi which has been proved.

When the verdict was called for, the Jury declined,
As the word was so puzzling to spell;
But they ventured to hope that the Snark wouldn't mind
Undertaking that duty as well.
So the Snark found the verdict, although, as it owned,
It was spent with the toils of the day:
When it said the word "GUILTY!" the Jury all groaned,
And some of them fainted away.

Then the Snark pronounced sentence,
    the Judge being quite
Too nervous to utter a word:
When it rose to its feet, there was
    silence like night,
And the fall of a pin might be heard.
"Transportation for life" was
    the sentence it gave,
"And *then* to be fined forty pound."
The Jury all cheered, though the
    Judge said he feared
That the phrase was not legally sound.

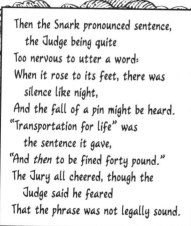

But their wild exultation was
    suddenly checked
When the jailer informed them,
    with tears,
Such a sentence would have
    not the slightest effect,
As the pig had been dead
    for some years.
The Judge left the Court,
    looking deeply disgusted:
But the Snark, though a little aghast,
As the lawyer to whom the
    defense was intrusted,
Went bellowing on to the last.

Thus the Barrister dreamed, while the bellowing seemed
To grow every moment more clear:
Till he woke to the knell of a furious bell,
Which the Bellman rang close at his ear.

Fit the Seventh
THE BANKER'S FATE

They sought it with thimbles, they sought it with care;
They pursued it with forks and hope;
They threatened its life with a railway-share;
They charmed it with smiles and soap.

And the Banker, inspired with a courage so new
It was matter for general remark,
Rushed madly ahead and was lost to their view
In his zeal to discover the Snark.

But while he was seeking with thimbles and care,
A Bandersnatch swiftly drew nigh
And grabbed at the Banker, who shrieked in despair,
For he knew it was useless to fly.

He offered large discount—he offered a cheque
(Drawn "to bearer") for seven-pounds-ten:
But the Bandersnatch merely extended its neck
And grabbed at the Banker again.

Without rest or pause—
    while those frumious jaws
Went savagely snapping around—
He skipped and he hopped, and he
    floundered and flopped,
Till fainting he fell to the ground.

The Bandersnatch fled as the others appeared
Led on by that fear-stricken yell:
And the Bellman remarked "It is just as I feared!"
And solemnly tolled on his bell.

He was black in the face, and they scarcely could trace
The least likeness to what he had been:
While so great was his fright that his waistcoat turned white—
A wonderful thing to be seen!

Down he sank in a chair—ran his hands through his hair—
And chanted in mimsiest tones
Words whose utter inanity proved his insanity,
While he rattled a couple of bones.

To the horror of all who were present that day,
He uprose in full evening dress,
And with senseless grimaces endeavoured to say
What his tongue could no longer express.

"Leave him here to his fate— it is getting so late!"
The Bellman exclaimed in a fright.
"We have lost half the day. Any further delay,
And we sha'n't catch a Snark before night!"

Fit the Eighth
THE VANISHING

They sought it with thimbles, they sought it with care;
They pursued it with forks and hope;
They threatened its life with a railway-share;
They charmed it with smiles and soap.

They shuddered to think that the chase might fail,
And the Beaver, excited at last,
Went bounding along on the tip of its tail,
For the daylight was nearly past.

"There is Thingumbob shouting!" the Bellman said.
"He is shouting like mad, only hark!
He is waving his hands, he is wagging his head,
He has certainly found a Snark!"

They gazed in delight, while the Butcher exclaimed
"He was always a desperate wag!"
They beheld him—their Baker—their hero unnamed—
On the top of a neighbouring crag,

Erect and sublime, for one moment of time.
In the next, that wild figure they saw
(As if stung by a spasm) plunge into a chasm,
While they waited and listened in awe.

"It's a Snark!" was the sound that first came to their ears,
And seemed almost too good to be true.
Then followed a torrent of laughter and cheers:
Then the ominous words "It's a Boo—"

Then, silence. Some fancied they heard in the air
A weary and wandering sigh
Then sounded like "—jum!" but the others declare
It was only a breeze that went by.

They hunted till darkness came on, but they found
Not a button, or feather, or mark,
By which they could tell that they stood on the ground
Where the Baker had met with the Snark.

In the midst of the word he was trying to say,
In the midst of his laughter and glee,
He had softly and suddenly vanished away —
For the Snark *was* a Boojum, you see.

Hunting the Snark with Pen and Ink

BY MAHENDRA SINGH

One afternoon a Christ Church mathematics tutor was taking a stroll when a curious and unexpected thought came to him, a random line of Nonsense verse that suddenly flashed through his mind:

"For the Snark *was* a Boojum, you see."

The day was July 18, 1874, and it had been nine years since the Reverend Charles Lutwidge Dodgson, under the pen name of Lewis Carroll, had published *Alice's Adventures in Wonderland* and three years since he had published *Through the Looking Glass*. Both books had been enormously popular, not only with children but also with the many adults who relished the sophisticated paradoxes and clever games of language, mathematics and logic with which the author had filled Alice's dream-like world. This style of literature was called Nonsense and Carroll was universally acknowledged to be its undisputed master.

He had written some poetry before that fateful morning (his *Jabberwocky* is a high point of *Through the Looking Glass*) but the verses which grew out of that single line were entirely different; they would become *The Hunting of the Snark*, the finest Nonsense poem ever written and an epic masterpiece which would fascinate readers and stir up more controversies and conflicting theories than anything else he ever wrote.

Carroll worked for two more years to finish the poem; he

couldn't stop himself from cramming more and more references into it, references to just about everything under the Victorian sun: English banking practices and naval history, sea-side bathing, life insurance policies, Shakespeare, music hall jokes and even billiards-playing. There were personal and professional references also: the Baker's boxes numbering 42, which was Carroll's age at the time; the Bellman's Rule of Three and the Beaver's Lesson which both seem to poke fun at Carroll's own profession of teaching mathematics to less than willing students. There were hints at contemporary events and culture: the Banker's Fate is an obvious parody of a Victorian minstrel show while the Barrister's Dream might refer to the trial of the Tichbourne Claimant (a notorious Australian swindler) or even the popular Gilbert and Sullivan operetta, *Trial by Jury*.

There was much in common with the *Alice* books; Carroll himself admitted that the Snark could be found on the same island where the Jabberwock had been slain. The *Snark* and the *Alice* books were equally populated by Bandersnatches and Jubjub birds and more importantly, the inhabitants all spoke the oddest sort of English full of ingenious portmanteau words (further explained in Carroll's Preface) such as beamish, frumious, galumphing and mimsy. Carroll labored hard to expand and improve upon *Alice's* Nonsense universe with even more impossible beasts and characters, all of them launched into galloping rhymes to chase after the Snark, faster and faster till the sudden, grim end.

And this is where Carroll departed from the *Alice* books, for although they also involved a quest, the hunt for the Snark was far darker. Perhaps the lunacy of the Mad Hatter's Party had finally taken over Carroll's Nonsense world, for it's clear that the Snark's hunters (most of them characters taken from everyday Victorian life) were not quite right in the head. Unable to count properly, going backwards with blank maps, chasing a mass delusion whilst armed with bits of paper, soap and eating utensils, things would only get worse and worse for them until one went utterly mad and another literally vanished away.

It was pretty strong stuff coming from a children's author such as Lewis Carroll, so much so that some critics still think the poem is best kept out of the hands of young people. But we know that Carroll did intend the poem to be read by both adults and children. In fact, the *Snark* was dedicated to a child, Gertrude Chataway; her name forms not only the first letter of each line but also the first word of each stanza of the dedicatory poem at the beginning of the book.

Carroll had a higher opinion of children's intelligence and curiosity than certain critics and he was confident that although some young people might not be interested in make-believe such as Snarks and Boojums and Bandersnatches, many others would be. He knew they would quickly understand that this was a kind of game of words and ideas with some very ingenious rules, complicated enough to challenge adults yet enjoyable enough to satisfy a curious child's sense of fun.

Certain critics also get quite worked up about the *Snark's* ultimate meaning. Naturally, most poems and books have some sort of meaning and the *Snark* is no different. The odd thing is that no one has ever quite figured out what it is (which may be part of the game, when one thinks about it). Curiouser and curiouser, we also know that whenever Carroll was asked what the poem meant, he always replied that he did not know. But as we've seen, the poem is full of all sorts of references to very real ideas, things and events and many readers have been tempted to solve the puzzle themselves by using these hints.

Some people believe that the poem is a satire on capitalism and its quest for wealth. Some think it is a self-portrait of Carroll himself. Others think it is about Christianity or philosophies such as Existentialism and Idealism. There are some who even think it's all about the colonization of Australia or Arctic exploration or even tuberculosis!

In any case, these controversies will go on forever, the *Snark* is that kind of story, so complicated and so full of riddles that just about any theory might fit to some degree. We should note that Carroll did admit in a letter to some children that he thought the meaning which *seemed* to fit the poem most beautifully was that it was an allegory of mankind's search for happiness.

Which finally brings us to this particular version of the *Snark*. It is a version illustrated with the techniques of Surrealism, a style of making art and literature which began in the aftermath of World War I, a time when many people were convinced that human nature itself must change if we were ever to be happy again after such an immense slaughter. The Surrealists hoped that by using the images and ideas of our dreams and our unconscious world to make art, they would awaken some dreamlike source of energy within their audience which might change the way they lived and worked and thought. They might learn to sleepwalk with their eyes wide open, so to speak, and then the world around them would slowly turn into a dream itself—a happy dream, hopefully!

The Surrealists thought very highly of Lewis Carroll and in particular his *Snark,* for it is a very Surrealist poem in the way it rearranges and distorts the real world according to half-hidden rules that seem based on the logic of dreams. And so I thought it best to use the techniques of Surrealism to illustrate my *Snark,* in particular the visual puns and riddles of such artists as Giorgio de Chirico, René Magritte, Alberto Savinio and Salvador Dalí.

But even the considerable resources of Surrealism were not sufficient to flesh out this *Snark.* I had to rummage through the entire history of art to explain certain verses, all the way from the Classical Rome of the Laocoön to the Late Medieval Flemish nightmares of Hieronymus Bosch and even the drawings of the Pre-Raphaelite artist, Henry Holiday, the original illustrator of the *Snark.* Our modern pop culture also proved useful. Look carefully and you'll spot references to the Fab Four and *The Hitchhiker's Guide to the Galaxy* and even to George Herriman's *Krazy Kat.* Some of the puns and puzzles that I used to expand and explain the verses are based on pertinent places and things and even foreign languages; I have to admit that the coincidence of the word "bander" in Bandersnatch also meaning "monkey" in Hindi was just too juicy to ignore!

In short, I've enjoyed making my little jokes and puzzles, just as much as Lewis Carroll enjoyed making his. I've tried not to cheat—each drawing should make some sort of sense of the verse it explains or at least, make Nonsense! And equally important, perhaps my readers, in particular the younger ones, will be intrigued enough by what they glimpse here to further pursue on their own that immense cultural heritage which silently—and so faithfully—awaits them.

ARTIST'S ACKNOWLEDGMENTS

My heartfelt thanks to the many Snark Hunters throughout the world who assisted, advised and encouraged me in my labors and researches; your names are too numerous to mention individually and an omission on my part would be inevitable and unforgivable. Particular thanks must go to the very kind and generous members and officers of the Lewis Carroll Society of North America, the staff of the *Knight Letter,* and above all, my very patient and beloved wife and muse, Farah.

ABOUT THE AUTHOR

Oxford University mathematics professor Charles Lutwidge Dodgson (1832–1898), under his pen name Lewis Carroll, created some of the most brilliant, original and uniquely inventive literature in the English language. He is most famous for three magical works: *Alice's Adventures in Wonderland, Through the Looking-Glass,* and the witty, whimsical and ever-elusive *The Hunting of the Snark.*

When pressed to explain the meaning of *The Hunting of the Snark,* Carroll invariably replied that he did not know. "I'm very much afraid I didn't mean anything but nonsense!" he wrote in a letter to friends, "Still, you know, words mean more than we mean to express when we use them: so a whole book ought to mean a great deal more than the writer meant. So, whatever good meanings are in the book, I'm very glad to accept as the meaning of the book. The best I've seen is...that the whole book is an allegory on the search for happiness. I think that fits beautifully in many ways."

ABOUT THE ARTIST

Mahendra Singh is an illustrator and longstanding Lewis Carroll aficionado. He is a member of the Lewis Carroll Society of North America and an editor for their journal, the Knight Letter. For Singh, creating the illustrations for *The Hunting of the Snark* "has been a labor of love — fitting Lewis Carroll into a proto-Surrealist straitjacket with matching Dada cufflinks."